A Table for One

Ms. Scott

MOLO GLOBAL
PUBLISHING

ISBN Paperback: 978-1-7350720-0-5

ISBN E-book: 978-1-7350720-3-6

Library of Congress Control Number: 2021902744

Published in the United States by Molo Global Publishing, an imprint of Molo Global Consulting, LLC, Maryland.

DEDICATION

For my grandmother Emma and my mother Elizabeth for creating a world with standards high enough to make me work hard but without boundaries to let me find my own way.
Grandma, I do miss you dearly. But although you're gone, I never have to wonder if you're proud because you always made sure that I knew that you were.
Thank you mama for giving me Roger and Kimberly and for creating children that are strong, resilient, and relentlessly loyal – just like you.

For every single person that ever poured into me in any way and in any measure.

For my Scott Girls, each of you already know that every last one of you are my favorite. Special thank you to Twylia for believing in the possibility of this book wayyy before I ever did. To Tierra, the best home healthcare nurse and brand visionary I know lol. And once again to Kimberly, my heart and my wings.

To Teria, because you know it all and still rock with me.
To my big little brother, Roger, because to you I am deserving of everything that is good.
To Ty, because you are you, and therefore always enough.

And for my very own Prince Amar…my reason.

TABLE OF CONTENTS

INTRODUCTION

HAPPINESS DEFINED is the experience of **a** love that courts you, nurtures you, and protects you, for no other reason than because you are you. It's the unrelenting presence of acceptance and commitment, even in those moments when one realizes that the content inside the package doesn't quite match the apparent perfection of the wrapping that surrounds it.

In other words, happiness is a process, not a feeling. It requires effort, not hope.

In order to thrive, happiness must be planted, grown, and nurtured from within. It cannot wait or beg for care from an external, and thus unreliable, steward.

Because in the end, if you don't take care of you – your happy – who will?

CHAPTER ONE

Mirror, mirror of my soul, what will it take to make me whole?

*H*ey there. Please allow me to introduce myself. I am Nia Elizabeth Hagins, Esquire. My friends and family call me Nia E. or just Nia. Some guys that I come across call me a 'lil baddie. A few of my exes call themselves fools. And oh yeah, the team over at the Hagins Family Law Office they call me the boss.

At five feet three inches and a hundred and thirty-three pounds, I can admit that sometimes it's hard to see me. But it's also never easy to ignore me when you do. Even when I say nothing, my milk chocolate skin, bright smile, glorious crown of sisterlocs, and 36in-28in-41in coke bottle frame says a whollleeee lot. This I know to be true.

I just turned 36 a couple of weeks ago. But you better believe it doesn't show. I find my way to my local gym five, if not six, days a week. I have a standing weekly 'pamper me' appointment with Ms. Janice for a full body deep tissue massage and facial. I keep my suits tailored, dresses fitted, and my heels on high. And this tailfeather still shakes just fine – if I do say so myself.

Yeah. To sum up my current situation, you can say that I'm single, successful… and empty.

That's right, on the outside I look like a whole lot of everything. But on the inside - on the inside - that's an entirely different story. Over the course of my life, I've let this state of emptiness become so familiar to me. It is my biggest shame. I am aware that everyone that sees me is probably convinced that I am confident and content. And I do absolutely nothing to correct this narrative that I've helped them create about me. I portray a vision of fullness. When in reality, I wouldn't know happy if it stood in front of me hitting the *woah* to a Megan Thee Stallion beat.

Let me be clear, my representative is worn out and in desperate need of a break.

But that's not even an option. If I dared to be authentic, present my true self, speak about my sadness

– the guilt would be swift and unrelenting. And ain't nobody got time for that! It's so true. The problem with having the appearance that you have it all together is that it's very hard to get permission from yourself, and from others, to not be okay; even though, sometimes, you are truly not okay. It's so much "easier" to be who I think that *they* expect me to be.

Oh boy, there I go sounding ungrateful again.

Listen, every corner of my life contains a blessing that I probably don't even deserve. Every single time adversity took its very best jab at my goals and aspirations, I either dodged the blow altogether or took the hit, fell down, and then had the audacity to get back up in even better condition than before I fell.

If I'm honest, sometimes I feel like there's a curse in resiliency. Like maybe I shouldn't bounce back, quite so fast. Or that I should find a way to permanently expose the scars that I know are there but that no one else can see. Who knew there was a wrong way to be blessed? Or that the price I'd pay for my spirit of gratitude was my ability to be outwardly vulnerable. I wish it was possible for those two feelings to coexist. That I could be grateful that I survived my trials but still have 'permission' to admit that I am fearfully aware of my flaws and yes, my inadequacies. I know, I know, blasphemous thoughts.

Don't get me wrong, surely I wouldn't want to change

my status as a 'conqueror' of adversity. And yes, success is definitely a beautiful thing. Even when it requires that I constantly portray a sense of togetherness that contradicts my actual state of fragmentation. Yet still, the ability to have the mental and physical fortitude to hold my own and thrive in a world that expects people that look like me to be 'less than' feels mighty damn good.

But what is success without balance? Call it a cliché but I am truly in love with my profession. I can say, without a shadow of a doubt, that the work I perform is the work God specifically designed me to do. And every single day I get the chance to make a real difference in someone's world.

My legal practice is three years old and sits in the middle of a community that is in the midst of change. Now mind you, this *'change'* probably feels like gentrification to the locals but is advertised as revitalization to the newcomers. *One day, in the not so distant future, I vow to run for city council to change the way this redevelopment process is perceived and implemented.*

But needless to say, my clients are diverse in terms of socioeconomic status, ethnicity, and cultural ties. When I say I represent all people, I mean ALL people. And I'm proud of that. I'm also proud of the respect that my name has in the community. You hear Nia

Elizabeth Hagins and you think of a winner (the words of the community, not mine – lest it sound as if I'm boasting). Although it is true, I can't help but to give my all to every single client that I represent - before, during and after trial. And more often than not, that dedication is rewarded with success: for my client, for my firm, and yes for my community.

I also make sure that the employees of the Hagins Family Law Office feel valued. There's no evidence of the 'angry black woman' at my firm. I create a work climate that underwrites honest mistakes, rewards innovation and creativity, and that allows each member of my staff to leave work at the office and to 'turn off' when we lock up the building at the end of each day. I make it a point to encourage them to always put their family and loved ones first, which ironically makes them even more committed to the success of my business.

But I do not practice what I preach. Not in the least. In fact, the closest I get to work life balance is looking at all of the family photos that my staff members have displayed on their desks or hung on their office walls.

Ok, crazy question alert. Do you ever feel like you'd give it all up just to be the "better half" to someone very special? No, just me? But seriously though, my best friend Jasmine always gives me the infamous side eye every time I tell her that I'm thinking about walking away. If not to be someone's better half, then to find my whole peace. I mean yes, my career is my pride and joy, but it does not fill me up. Some people are lucky to have them both: success and fullness. I am not a member of that squad.

Nevertheless, I still can't shake Luna (short for Lunatic). She's this small (aggravating) creature that has a permanent residence in the back of my mind. I'm thoroughly convinced that her only purpose in life is to remind me that I have an *obligation* to be happy. And every single time I feel a sensation other than joy, like loneliness for example, she kicks me...hard. And that little heifer is strong. And I know for a fact that she never sleeps.

Meanwhile, I've spent the better part of my life, waiting on the official diagnosis that I am in fact, allergic to happiness. I mean, seriously, what other possible explanation can there be?

I am bosom buddy, BFF, sister wife to the façade or representative of happy. Indeed, that's my ride or die. But the real thing, the actual Queen of Peace and Joy...well, I can't say that we've ever truly met.

That probably explains why my relationship with love is so toxic.

Through the years, I've found that the worst part of love is when it isn't returned. Especially from the person who I saw looking back at me in the mirror.

For the longest time, her eyes never lit up with appreciation or smiled as a sign of endearment, as she stared at me. So that became my standard – or lack thereof – for every person that I encountered. I wonder what would've happened if I'd required the person that knew me the best, to also love me the most? Instead of expecting someone who would only know what I desired to share, to somehow manage to adore me with pure and reckless abandon.

Surprisingly enough, that hasn't worked out well for me.

It is truly so ironic. Every single time that I love, I love deeply! But all the while I am so committed to this other person, to building this external relationship, I am so unkind to myself. And I absolutely refuse to do the work I know I need to do to repair my heart. How can a heart that is broken from the inside out love anyway?

But enough of all of that, I've got to get ready for a date with Khari. And let me tell you, Khari is definitely the one.

CHAPTER TWO

EXPECTATIONS

Plant me in a space where I can fly
Create in you a sanctuary that I can explore
Forget that mine is a love you already have
Give me all I need knowing I'll require more

Show me what it's like to feel safe
Break a pattern of pain that existed before you
Commit to our forever one day at a time
Put in more work when it seems there's nothing left
to do

Be a provider of passion and peace
Hold me when we're a thousand miles apart
Remind me of the joy I've never felt
And that for every journey we end, there's a new one
    to start

Plant me in a space where I can grow
Root me in a love where I can still soar
Forget that my love belongs exclusively to you
Be all that I need knowing I may require more

Plant me in a space where I can fly

How I Know

*H*e makes me feel like I'm enough
Even while he encourages me to be better
He reminds me that limits are distractions
And that my only real goal is not settle

I could crawl inside his skin, his soul
And still feel like I'm too far away
Short months will turn into long years
And I'll still crave him like I do on this very day

He's showing me the power in patience
Revealing that true love is created, not felt
And this is how I know that after him
There will be no one else

Khari Wright is amazing. Khari is life. Khari is my everything. I love Khari, deeply. However, Khari does not feel the same way about me. To me, Khari is the whole entire universe. To Khari, I'm just a couple of planets....on some days, maybe a galaxy.

But that's neither here nor there.

I'll tell you that the very moment that I saw this person, my heart threw up the white flag. It made a public service announcement to all that would listen that I was officially out of the game. Every single thing that I imagined I ever wanted or needed in a partner, I knew that I'd found it in Khari. These were all the thoughts roaming in my head, in my heart, throughout my body... and Khari and I had not even spoken yet.

It should go without saying that an untamed heart is a very dangerous weapon. This is a lesson I'd already learned, or shall I say, already been exposed to since clearly, I had not learned. And yet, I continued to let my emotions lead me places to which my heart had not been invited, and as such, my love had no place being.

And so I will confess, Khari never courted me.

I courted him fiercely though, from the very beginning. And I now realize that this is the reason that we were doomed, from the very beginning. I never gave him the chance to make up his own mind about me. I was too busy trying to convince him that I was the woman he should choose as his Queen. I did not consider that maybe his kingdom was already complete. Maybe it was not his season for courtship. Maybe he had healing to do. Maybe, just maybe, my persistence disrupted his process.

But don't be confused. Without knowing it, Khari definitely led me on. Every single time that man looked at me, I saw and felt nothing but adoration. Felt it melt through my skin, travel through my veins, and settle in my soul. Khari's eyes disrupted his process as well. They never got the word that this was not his season, our season, for love.

I get it now though. It's so possible for a man to recognize the quality of a woman, respond accordingly, and still not choose her. He can admire her essence and still have absolutely no desire to move towards a union. This is indeed a thing, a possibility.

But because I did not require Khari's courtship and skipped right to our companionship, I did not allow myself the time and space to discern his intent.

Or notice when he never expressed it. Instead, I recognized just enough of the positive signs to justify a premature and inaccurate conclusion that we wanted the same things. Which allowed me to readily ignore all the obvious signs that we did not.

But again, all of that is neither here nor there.

What to wear? What to wear? What to wear? Tonight Khari is taking me to dinner at Georgia Brown's on 15th street. It's my favorite place to eat in all of D.C. and Khari knows that. Awwwww, what can I say? He's so attentive to me - to the things that I like, the things that I need and the desires of my heart. I'd say that he's the perfect example of when something walks like a duck and quacks like a duck but is definitely not a duck. Meaning, every interaction that Khari has with me, exemplifies love, but Khari does not love me. A goat, yep, not a duck, Khari is definitely a goat.

You wanna know something asinine, insanely crazy? I find myself blaming him for not loving me. In other words, I manage to find fault in him for something that I was already guilty of-and had been for years. I wonder if he senses the lack of connection I have with my own self-worth which in turn causes his own hesitation. It's kind of like...kind of like a mortgage company that requires a potential homeowner to pay a small down payment up front. Rightfully so, before the lender enters into this 30 year contract for a vastly more substantial amount, they want a small reassurance that the borrower has a vested interest in the transaction. Replace lender with suitor. Replace contract with relationship. Replace 30 years with a lifetime. And there you have it. How crazy is it for me to expect my desired suitor to willingly risk the forfeiture of his own vulnerabilities and the foreclosure of his already strained emotions, when I can't even bring my own endorsement to the table?

It's real funny how crazy works.

It goes without saying that everything the Creator does is intentional. But that becomes even more obvious when I think about the two separate terms that join together to become relation + ship. I've come to believe that it is the strength of an individual's internal *relation*s that serves as the **anchor** to keep the romantic *ship* afloat: when the waters are still and definitely when they become turbulent. In the absence of that self-love, it becomes too much added weight for the other partner to bear alone, and not surprisingly, the *relationship*... sinks.

It's pretty ironic now, but in hindsight I think that is why courtship is so important. Courtship is when investments are made. The truth is that it was unrealistic for me to expect Khari to become vested in a relationship that required no effort from him. Conversely, the act of courting would've required an abundance of action, effort, and initiative of his own accord. And it probably would've increased the likelihood, although never provided a guarantee, that he would have put forth the attention and action required to sustain the relationship – if only to get the maximum return on his 'courtship investment'.

And that is why I must become intimately acquainted with the act of *self*-courtship. And also why I must require proper courting from my future, potential suitors.

But for now, I hear a knock on my front door. Khari is always so punctual.

————————

And fine. Khari is definitely fine. I can't help but admire the beauty of this vision seated across from me. Khari's an accomplished businessman that keeps his swagger turned all the way up to one thousand trillion. He's a successful broker and also owns several parking garages in strategic, high traffic, areas throughout the DMV. It's far from an understatement when I say that this man makes money in his sleep. Which is icing on an already delectable cake.

For dinner tonight, I decided on this tight denim dress that accentuated my own Georgia peach and nonexistent waist. Khari is wearing dark jeans and this plaid burgundy button up that makes me want to do some very strange things to him…later that is.

"Did you hear me Nia?"

"I'm sorry what did you say love? I got distracted looking at you". *I swear I can flirt with this man all night long.*

"You're funny," he says as he smiles ear to ear. *Puddy in my hands.* "I asked you if you're getting the crab cakes and sweet potato fries again tonight?"

"Of course I am handsome. I honestly didn't know there were other items on the menu."

"You're too much woman."

"And I know that you know just how much woman I am."

I did say that I could flirt with this man alllll night long right?

Khari and I are seated across from each other in an intimate corner of the restaurant. And under the table, I can't stop myself from tracing hearts on his knee with my fingertip.

Secretly, I'm dreading the conversation I'm about to start because I know the whole entire mood is about to shift. But it's unavoidable. Khari's leaving the country on a business trip in a couple of days. He'll be gone for three weeks. And call me petty, but I want to make sure he has plenty to think about on that long flight and while he's away.

"Khari. Baby, you know I love you right?"

"Of course I know that."

"Baby, how do you feel about me?"

"What are you talking about?" And there's the shift.

"Khari, you know exactly what I mean. How do you *feel* about *me*?"

"I don't know Nia. I don't know."

And there you have it. The exact moment that I felt the impact of a ten ton truck as it dropped directly onto my heart from the highest point on planet Earth. *Play it cool Nia. Do not cause a scene. After all, you got stuff to lose.*

"Really Khari, you don't know? Then why are we here?" Surprisingly, I haven't raised my voice. And it doesn't sound like I'm crying the river that's flooding my insides. But you better believe I'm not tracing any more hearts on this man's knee.

"What do you mean Nia?"

"I mean…why do you date me so intently, cater to me so deliberately? Why are you sitting across from me like there's no other place you'd rather be? Why in the world do you act like all you care about is pleasing me…making me smile…making sure that I'm happy? And all the while, you have no idea how you feel about me. How is that even possible Khari? How?"

"I guess… I guess I just don't think like that. I just take it one day at a time. I live in the moment and I don't really think about my feelings."

Damn. Why in the hell did of all these trucks pick this exact moment to start falling out of the sky – on me?

"Khari, I'm gonna get up from this table now. And I'm gonna walk out that door. Don't worry, I'll get myself home. I need you to know that when I get up from this table, I'm done with all of this. I'm done with us. What am I even talking about, there is no us? You've made that so very clear. Your heart never has been and never will be available to me. I fully accept that now. You are an amazing man and I don't have a single bad thing to say about you. But I just can't continue in this emotion-less situation. You are incapable of feeling – this I know to be true."

"But Khari, I take complete ownership of this. Because when we started this thing, I placed myself behind the steering wheel and allowed you to ride shotgun. Even though it was never my place to drive. I'm supposed to be sitting cute in the passenger seat preparing to respond accordingly when you ask me important questions like. 'Hey beautiful, what do you think about us shifting gears from just being friends to being exclusive?' Or how about, 'My love, it crossed my mind that maybe we should set our final destination towards the alter, is that ok with you?'"

"Clearly I didn't arrive at this revelation quick

enough. But the final act I will do from behind the wheel, is to move this wreck of an entanglement to the side of the road. I'm done. Good-bye Khari."

And with that, I got my fine ass up, put an extra switch in my hips, and walked out that door.

Damn, I should've at least waited until the food came out.

CHAPTER THREE

VICE VERSA

*E*very time I see love
The nerves in my skin, rejoice
The switch behind my pupils, flips to on
The shape of my lips form a curve, towards heaven
And every fairytale I don't believe in, becomes my
   absolute truth
And every time love sees me
His experience is the same

PURE

*W*henever you touch me
I experience the most natural elements of joy
You look at me in a way that rebuilds all the hopes of
forever
That my old life tried to destroy

Yet I'm terrified of the way I feel for you
Of the control you have on my peace
I could try and go forward without you
But even the thought of that makes me weak

Besides, I am my best self when I'm with you
You are the man I always deserved, but never knew
I'm convinced that I was made to be the woman at
your side
And that you are the reason the last love I planted
never grew

My destiny is connected to you
Of that, I'm completely and utterly sure
Since there's no way an end could ever come
To a bond that is this powerful, this pure

And let the floodgates open...

So, I think the reason that this hurts the way it does, is, because it's like, in one sense, the not knowing, you know was hard. But now I know, and I can't unknow it. And that, that hurts as well.

I won't say that it hurts worse, because...in the end, I needed to know. And so, I'm glad, I'm like, really really really really really glad.

And, you know, it hurts because, how do you spend as much time as we've spent together. And mind you, I know, it has been a great deal of distance. I'm not going to discount that. But how do you spend as much time, as we HAVE, spent together, and feel nothing? How are you not any closer to knowing, how you feel about me, than you were years ago?

I mean, it just feels like, I made it all up. It feels like, I can't trust, myself. I can't trust my feelings. I can't trust my heart. Because I created this entire relationship, with somebody, who just doesn't care. Doesn't care at all. Doesn't care at all.

And you know, he can say that he doesn't care. He can say that his feelings aren't there. But I didn't make it up. I didn't make it up.

So how is it that, on one end, that you can look at me

like I'm your whole world. But when it comes time to speak about you, you can say that you don't think about it, or that you're not emotionally available. Or, you're used to being alone. And speak, in no way, shape or form, about any connection that you have with me. Any feelings that you have for me. How?

I mean, it makes it impossible, to want him. Like, to want him at this point, is to say, you know, I want somebody who's made it abundantly clear – abundantly clear – that this is going nowhere. Where he is, is where he's going to stay.

So, what do I do? I gotta allow myself to just sit in the pain. To forgive myself, for falling for someone, who I knew from the very, very beginning, was not emotionally available. And for believing that time, would make him feel what, how, I feel for him. And for believing that if he could, if he was willing, to feel half of what I feel, we would be ok. But he isn't.

So, I'm not saying that I'm done with love. I just know that it's not worth it. It's not worth, this, moment. If this is what love gets you, I don't want it, with anybody.

I just want to be alone. I just wanna be alone.

Now when I talk to him, when I see him again. Because I will talk to him again, I will see him again. I have to do something that's very unnatural. And that's pretend that I don't love him. That I don't want him.

I just have to accept the fact that it's not meant for me.

Love is not meant to me.

And so how do I make solitude bearable? How I do make being alone…enough?

The pain that comes with the loss of Khari's presence is unbelievable. It is a mind numbing…heart numbing…unbelievable   pain.

But nevertheless, it is a pain that I can bury and from which I can move on. It is not one in which I will wallow or to which I will sacrifice my peace.

In my heart, I allowed myself to go back to that table at Georgia Brown's. To sit down and to finish that conversation with Khari.

And as I allowed the tears to leave my eyes, I said to my love, "All I ever wanted was you. Just as you are. Nothing more, nothing less, just you. But I also wanted you to crave the sound of my voice, the sight of my face, for no other reason than because it was a Tuesday. Not a special day by anybody's measure - just a regular old, boring old Tuesday."

"And I blamed myself, for not letting the awesomeness of who you are – without those cravings – be enough for me. For us. Because there is no doubt in my mind, or even in my heart, that you would move heaven and earth for me. I know that you do think of me, way more than we speak. That you do long for me, way more than you show up. But I also know that you are not capable of closing the gap – between what we are and what we could be."

"And so I give myself permission to walk away from your…from our…potential. To realize that it is okay that our desires will not meet, in this season or in our lifetime. That you can keep your crown, and that I can straighten mine, even as we create our dynasties apart. We will not lose our individual values, even though we will not build on our worth as a team."

And in my heart, Khari said back to me, "Nia, every single thing that you felt in your soul, and that I failed to say or show, is still our truth. I always saw us when I looked at you. And that's why you would always see that smile. And even though I do believe that one day I can be open to the expressions of love and adoration that you need, I can also admit that 'one day' is not this day. If losing you…this…is the price I have to pay for the resistance of my heart, just know that it is a debt that I will never fully repay. And because of that, I cannot accept your good-bye Nia, I never will. With us, there will always be a later."

"Khari, if it's possible to not spend one more second waiting for you and still pray that you end up as my forever, then that is where I am. If you see me by myself, know that I am not alone. The crazy thing is that, if you'd loved me right, I wouldn't be forced to do my work. Nor would you be forced to do yours. And so, while I initially buckled under the pain of not having you, in the end I thank your heart for not being available."

"I also recognize that I never offered you an incentive to join me in love since I gave you all the benefits of my heart and didn't require you to do anything to earn it. Don't get me wrong, in no way do I think that you took advantage of me or the situation. At the same time, I do think you exploited the opportunity to have the devotion and affection of a woman that you always wanted without having to fix the part of yourself that could not return it."

"Nia, if it's possible to not expect you to wait but still hope that you're here when my love evolves naturally, then that is where I am. I do not want another woman. And I know it seems that I'm not capable, but I do believe that I can fall in love. And just know that I plan to, with you."

CHAPTER FOUR

J could never be my best self with you
Yet for years it was only you, that I desired
Until I could no longer stand the smell
of death
Coming from within
My soul

Still I thought you were life, and that I was wrong
I grew familiar with feeling less than my worth
Allowed myself to be temporarily reassured
When you did the things you were supposed to

Because you did them
So infrequently

The brutal truth is that I never really loved you
Nor you me
But together, we never had to change
You accepted me broken
And preferred that I stay that way
So that I could stay
With you

But a day came when I decided to soar
Above the familiar, to a better version of life
That could not include you, me
And peace

Yet I can admit, leaving us hurt in the worst way
That is, until I got used to the sensation of joy
As it traveled unrestrained
Within my soul

KONCRETE ROSE

Let me be clear
Just because I don't require your validation

Does not mean that I'm conceited, and
Just because I can do without the games and lies
Doesn't mean that a real King isn't needed

See, I'm that sister keeping court behind the 10 foot
    wall
Weary of any soul that attempts to break through
I can appreciate all of your attention and intentions
But breaking my heart, is what you not gone do

They say, you only live once
But that's if, you've never cheated death
And emerged no longer willing to compromise the
    presence
Of both peace of mind and good health

So I'm protective of my space, my goods, my sanity
Ever mindful of how many different ways the winds of
    love can blow
And I have no issue waiting for a King
That can handle the beauty and thorns of a Koncrete
    Rose

HUES OF FIERCENESS

Make no mistake about it
Every shade of the black woman is fierce
She is made in every hue of Queen
Whether the crown atop her head is adorned with
the straightest strands or the tightest coils, she is
beauty.
She is a vision in her inches or locs
She is majestic when shaven
And the evidence of goddess is clearly woven
throughout the intricacies of her headwrap

She is fierce in every element of her complexity
And in every hue of her complexion

She's not "pretty for a dark-skinned girl"
Or "bad" because she's a "redbone".
She is phenomenal, just because she IS.
She is fierce just in her existence.
And make no mistake about it,
You can neither add to, or subtract from, her worth
for any reason

I struggled with the idea of seeking therapy again. Not because I doubted whether or not I needed it. Trust me, that is one fact that is not debatable. I think I just generally feel that my problems aren't real enough. In fact, I once had a therapist tell me that she had clients with "real problems" and the ones I described to her did not even come close.

I can't say for sure that is where I first experienced the guilt of my issues, but I can say that is when I began to justify that guilt.

Dr. Jill's office is the definition of serene. Which is actually kind of funny, because she has a way of making me step all the way out of my comfort zone to achieve levels of emotional and mental accountability that I always tried to avoid. She believes in me and all that I can become. And she is determined to make me get out of my own way – to help me become comfortable in the role as my number one fan and give up my title as my own worst enemy.

So here we go. Another round in the ring: Old me vs. Best me.

"Nia, tell me something that you love about yourself." Classic Dr. Jill. No formalities, straight to the point. Clearly, she takes the healing business very seriously.

"Ok, let me see. I love that God made me simple. In theory, my thresholds for satisfaction and happiness are very low. Which is so ironic because, in practice, I am very seldom satisfied – or happy."

"You didn't answer my question Nia. Tell me about a quality that you possess that makes you glad that you're not somebody else, that makes you pleased to be exactly who you are, in this moment."

"It sounds like such a simple question Dr. Jill. And I really don't know why it's so hard to answer. Let me try again."

"Just take a deep breath. Close your eyes. Focus on you. Listen to your heart. Find that thing that brings a smile to your face. And describe it to me."

So I did that. I sat up straight. I inhaled, then slowly exhaled. I closed my eyes. I crossed my arms and begin to rub my fingertips up and down my bare arms. I felt my heart jump and then the smile that began to tug at the corners of my lips. I tried to focus on the reason for the tug, that jump. And I found it. "Dr. Jill, I love that I am passionate. I love that I don't know how to not be 'all in' when it comes to the things and people that I care about. I think that's a blessing. That is a quality that I would not change."

"Ok. Good. Much better. Now how did you let the very thing that you love about yourself, become the source of so much of your pain?" Well damn. I say again, classic Dr. Jill.

"Wow. I did do that, didn't I?"

"Yes. Yes, you did. You took something meant for your good and turned it into a weapon used to break you. And I'm gonna tell you why I think that happened. You are not discriminate with your passion Nia. You give it away. You don't recognize it as the prized possession that it is. Because along with that passion, comes your time, your thoughts, your energy, and almost certainly – your heart. The things that you should be the most protective of, you give away. Why is that Nia?"

"Honestly, Dr. Jill, for most of my life, the idea of being alone brought so much sadness to my heart. There were times that I seriously preferred the state of death to the thought of being stuck with myself. I found no value in simply being me. I've always had this deep fear that I'm not good enough. And because of that fear, I always find myself trying to convince others that I am. So yes, I am extremely indiscriminate with my passion. Even a bit reckless if I wanna keep it all the way real. But I truly believe that once I train myself how to behave as if I'm good enough…exactly as I am – then I can finally get out of the convincing business."

"Nia, what I hear you saying is that every time somebody comes into contact with you, you immediately give them the unfair, unachievable, task of saving you. You immediately make it their responsibility to complete you. And when they inevitably fail at a mission-that was never supposed to be theirs to carry out-you have the audacity to be hurt."

"Listen Nia, you have to remove all that pressure that you place on the people in your life and on your relationships, so that you can do a better job of protecting yourself, from yourself. I hate to be the one to tell you this, but the only person you can ever hold accountable, for your own happiness, is that beautiful brown skinned woman you see staring back at you in the mirror."

"Teach your inner voice to be kind, to be adoring, to be complementary, to be compassionate, to be intentional and consistent with her praise, to be understanding and forgiving when you make your mistakes. All those things that you want from another human, teach it and expect it from 'her' first."

"I know you're right Dr. Jill. I know you're right."

"Nia, it's not even about whether or not I'm right or if you're wrong. What I'm telling you right now is a matter of necessity. You've got to go about making this change with a sense of urgency. Like the state of your present and future happiness depends on it. Like severing the hold that your old emotional, mental, and even physical bad habits have on you, is your number one priority. Because it is. Right now you're standing in front of a glass door. And on the other side of that door is the best version of you. Your ability to get the key to open that door is tied to your willingness to do your own work. Now, are you gonna just stand there and look at that woman you've always known you could be? Or are you gonna do the work, get a hold of that key, and literally unlock the door to your very best life."

"I will do my work Dr. Jill. Mainly because I want a different outcome than the one I always get when I jump from one 'real' love to the next 'real' love and never make a pit stop to focus on 'self' love. I want to be in that space where love doesn't have a timeline. Where I don't get anxious if the person I'm interested in doesn't immediately return the same sentiment. I want to get to a place where the love from another person actually comes as a surprise because I've been so busy loving on myself to notice they were even falling for me, until the moment they express that they did in fact, fall for me."

"Nia, what you just described is the state of life as it should be. In fact, what if I told you that the Creator gave you just enough time, talent, and passion to fulfill your intended purpose on earth – the one He gave you before you were even born? And every single moment that you waste looking for things he already equipped you with, you miss out on more day, one more opportunity, to fully live out your purpose. And in the end, it's not even worth it. You don't gain a single thing from chasing love, meanwhile you've deprived someone in the world – if only yourself- of the opportunity to discover the reason you were put here to begin with."

"Do your work Nia, for the sake of us all. But especially for you."

CHAPTER FIVE

CAPE

Who gave me this thing in the first place
That is the question of the hour
Who tricked me into believing that if I put this thing on
It would give me all this so called 'magic' and power

In reality, I'm NOT your super woman
You didn't see my fall but I'm definitely still kneeling
Under the pressure of trying to be everything you expect

While paying no attention to the hell that I'm feeling

But right now, I'm feeling like enough is enough
That gaining your approval is not worth losing my peace
In fact, what if I confessed to you that I'm hurting
Inflicted by the kind of pain the eyes could never see

But that, that's something that I can change
And I know exactly what it is that I have to do
And I won't apologize for doing what's necessary for me
Even if it means I have to inconvenience you

So don't call me, don't text me
And whatever you do, do not come by
Because the super woman that you've become so accustomed to
Just hung up an out of office sign

Don't ask me how long I'll be gone
I can only tell you as long as it takes
Until it's safe to be a regular 'ole' phenomenal woman
And not a superhero wearing your cape

I finally realize that I have to be kind to myself, first, and always. And that one of the biggest ways that I can demonstrate this commitment to self-kindness is in finding work-life balance. I now acknowledge that careers are designed as a way to realize a dream-for those of us that are blessed in that way-but were never intended to satisfy that innermost desire to be and feel full. That fullness is the outcome of work alright, but not the work we do for others, but the result of the effort and energy we devote to ourselves. And we have to be very careful about protecting that energy…and renewing that energy, as needed.

And so, I've come to the conclusion that I have to develop the habit of doing or saying things that make me say, 'Thank you self.' And that I should do or say this thing at least once a day, every day, without fail. In theory, this shouldn't be hard a task to complete. After all, it's not like the concept of saying 'Thank you' is in any way foreign to me. As a southern belle, my mama definitely raised me to be polite to others. No, it's the placement of the word 'Self' at the end that is new. In hindsight, I can see that this is that thing, the act of being kind to yourself, that my mama did not teach me. And that with time, I did not properly teach myself.

The reality of it all is that the only person that can love me EXACTLY how I want to be loved, is the pretty brown skinned woman I see looking back at me in the mirror. In the end, she is the only person that literally knows what's going on inside of my head. And though I've allowed her to get away from this responsibility, she is the person who has the access and capacity to be the most responsive to not only what I need, but also 'when' I need it and can deliver it 'how' I need it. Anybody else can only give me their best effort. And because they are human, they will always inevitably fail, in some measure, at fulfilling the desires of another person.

My mission is to create and maintain that state of satisfaction and fullness, by and with myself.

For example, I know without a shadow of a doubt that the sight of purple tulips makes me smile from the inside out. And I also know that as a successful attorney, I am in fact a woman of means that can afford as many purple tulips as I desire. As such, I will make it a new habit to routinely treat myself to purple tulips. And when I do so, I will say, "Thank you, Self."

And when I'm able to make the curls of my hair lay just so or I notice just how pretty my brown eyes really are, I will say to myself, "Hey beautiful." And then I will respond, "Thank you, Self."

And yes, even when I indulge in a really long, extra bubbly, and selfishly soothing bubble bath, I will whisper out loud - just slightly louder than the relaxing classical tunes or soft R&B hits - "Thank you, Self."

And you know what, I also decided to change the station inside my heart. That's right, I'm officially tired of hearing the same old love songs. If it doesn't uplift me, I don't play it. If it doesn't make me feel like the finest thing walking the face of God's green earth, I don't listen. If the sound of the lyrics don't cause me to smile uncontrollably from ear to ear, it's not a tune on my playlist. Period.

In fact, the new Nia now knows that, at its core, love is easy. Especially when it originates from within. No one has the power to take me low, because I'm now at one with happy and allergic to pain. Hurt is a fact of life, I know this. But pain, pain is something I can control, especially the kind that threatens my inner peace. That pain, I will no longer allow. I will not only control the kind of things and thoughts that have the power to trigger that kind of a detrimental response, I will also ensure that only a very, very select few people have access to the knowledge of those triggers.

Indeed, one thing that I failed to realize, until now, is that I am the end game. Not an 'us' scenario. Not marriage, just me. The work that I need to do is necessary not so that I can be suitable for a union, but so that I can be content in solitude.

My peace equation looks something like this:

My Happiness + The Fulfillment of My Purpose = The

Creation and Sustainment of My Peace.

No other human is a factor in that equation. No other action, or lack thereof, is a factor. My happiness, my purpose, my peace. The end game.

I must admit that it is such a blessing to get to a place where I can be alone and not feel like a single thing – or person – is missing. I can feel the sensation of 'enoughness' based solely in my own presence. Admittedly, I've never ever felt this way. And it feels amazing. And dare I say it, worth the wait.

Siri, play Mary J. Blige 'Work That.'

It's finally date night again. I received an invitation from the most beautiful trio of people I know – me, myself and I. That's right, this morning I said to myself, *"Nia, I'm taking you out lady. I see you working hard, doing so much good for everyone else. So much so that tonight, I just wanna spoil you."*

Do whatever you need to do to make sure you look your absolute finest, but we have a reservation at Georgia Brown's tonight. I called up the General Manager, our Soror Patrice, and she's gonna make sure we have a seat with the very best view in the house. And don't worry, I made sure to tell her that the most special guest of the evening, will only require 'A Table for One'."

And with a smile, spanning from ear to lovely ear, I happily said, "Thank you...Self."

COMING NEXT....

Wow, that just happened. I just concluded a meeting with a few of my closest colleagues and friends and informed them of my intent to run for public office later this year. Every last one of them provided their unequivocal endorsement and pledged their support, both in time and financial contributions, to my future campaign.

Don't get me wrong, I am passionate about law and running my practice is extremely rewarding. However, building neighborhoods that provide economic, educational, social, and cultural enrichment to local residents and that are also sustainable and accessible to all – that is the thing that makes my heart smile. I can't believe that soon I'll actually get to do both, practice law and be a leader and practitioner in the field of community development. Oh yes, you better believe I'm already claiming victory over that election! I happen to know that community initiatives and priorities are a direct reflection of the interests of those elected to represent those communities, not necessarily the desires of the residents. Especially not the needs of those citizens that are disenfranchised and that are thought to be voiceless and thus powerless. I vow to be a representative of all, but I will definitely be an advocate for them. There I go, strategizing for a position that I don't even hold...yet.

As it happens, I'm scheduled to speak at a local fundraiser to build a much-needed community center in a few weeks. Terrance Anderson is one of the people I invited over for the announcement of my future campaign. He's already on the City Council so I valued his insight on both my suitability and my 'electability.' He is also a mutual friend that I share with Khari. On his way out of the meeting, Terrance made it a point to let me know that Khari would be at the community center fundraiser.

When I slyly asked Terrance if Khari would have a date, he looked at me like I'd actually sprouted a second head right in front of his face. He then shook his head and said, "Both of ya'll are crazy." I couldn't help but to laugh out loud. Like many of our friends, Terrance is convinced that Khari and I belong together.

But that's neither here nor there...at least not in this moment.

I can't lie though, it's exciting to know that Khari will be there. A lot has changed for me, and within me, since me we last spoke or saw each other. And I do wonder if my heart will still smile when he looks at me or if his eyes will still light up as they seem to do, only when I'm within his sight.

But I can tell you this, even if Khari still isn't ready to view me as more than a galaxy, he will surely see that I'm already the brightest star in my own universe. Indeed, maybe there's still space for him in my world, and then again, maybe there's not....

E A S Y

Loving me is like putting one foot in front of the
    other
An action he does without thought
He provides for me as if his sole purpose in life
Is to free my cares before they're ever caught

He holds me while we sleep
As if I'm a dream he won't let escape
His touch is a vow of loyalty that sends
A chill up my spine and a smile to my face

If there's ever a choice between what he said
    and they said
Then that's the easiest decision I'll ever make
The security he gives me is a priceless gift
And I'll always take his word straight to the bank

Oh to be loved by a King
Who values my happiness above all else
A man that will live out the remainder of his days
Making sure love is the easiest joy I've ever felt

ABOUT THE AUTHOR

OCTAVIA SCOTT is a native of Sylvania, Georgia. She earned a Bachelor of Arts degree in Political Science from Agnes Scott College in Decatur, Georgia and a Master of Public Administration from Marist College (Poughkeepsie, New York). Octavia started her current career as a commissioned officer in the United States Army over eighteen years ago. She founded her first organization Scott Village, LLC in 2020. Octavia is also the founder of Pamper. Purpose. Service., LLC, an organization that strives to normalize the importance of self-care, self-kindness and self-love. Her website, pamperpurposeservice.com is projected to launch in April 2021.

Octavia is currently stationed in Pyeongtaek, South Korea. She has one son, Amar.

Made in the USA
Las Vegas, NV
13 March 2021

19472615R00035